VENI
VIDI
VICI
ARMANI
FENDI
GUCCI

"LITTLE MISS MARY AND THE BIG MONSTER MAKEOVER"
Published by Next Line Publishing. First publication in Great Britain.
ISBN: 978-0-9554941-0-9

www.nextline.com

Printed in Poland
EUROPRODUCTION Sp. z o.o.
www.europroduction.pl

LITTLE MISS MARY
AND THE BIG MONSTER MAKEOVER

WORDS & PICTURES BY G.G. TOROPOV & CLEONE CASSIDY

www.littlemissmary.com

LITTLE MISS MARY was tired from shopping –
All day on her feet she'd been merrily hopping
From boutique to salon, from one to the other,
While asking for THIS and for THAT from her Mother...

"I want to have this and I want to have that!
Those shoes that I bought will look nice with that hat.
My open-toed sandals are just, SOOO passé!
If I wear them to school, what WILL the girls say?

I need a new skirt, and a dress, and a jacket,
For tennis, new trainers to match my new racket,
New t-shirt. New blouse. A new Fendi bag –
The one on display, with a WHOPPING price tag!"

Little Miss Mary's Mummy was proud,
She TOO always spent to the limit allowed
On the gold credit card, which her husband had given –
She KNEW her excesses would soon be forgiven.

Little Miss Mary was a chip off the block,
If she could shop, she would shop and right round the clock!
Three-sixty a year and twenty-four-seven,
Impressive for someone who just turned eleven...

But hardly a coup, when all POSH Mummies coo,
Into Porsche baby prams: "Gucci-goo, Gucci-goo."
No wonder that Mary's first words to her nanny
Were: "Pla-da, Ga-ba-na, La-cwa" and "A-ma-ni!"

"Moschino? Versace? Where SHALL we go next?"
"That's enough for today, you maxed-out the AmEx.
Any more shopping must wait till tomorrow,
There's plenty more money that Daddy can borrow."

On hearing the news Mary drew a deep sigh:
"But there's SOOO much more that I wanted to buy.
Sooo many shoes that I kept a keen eye on,
Sooo many dresses I wanted to try on."

But Mummy had already summoned assistants,
Who replied to her call in no more than an instance.
In a blink of an eye they were all in position,
Eager to please (as they worked for commission).

They loaded their bags in the big four-by-four.
They filled up the boot and they covered the floor,
Till there was no space left, no place left to pack –
So they piled even MORE bags above the ski-rack.

And off home they drove – Mother and Daughter
Hydrating themselves with Evian water;
Mum at the wheel of her new Chelsea Tractor,
Miss Mary behind her, poised to distract her...

With pertinent problems like: "How can one tell,
Between bags that are bootleg and REAL Chanel?"
Or questions like: "Mum, why don't WE have a butler?"
And other BIG issues from Vogue and from Tatler.

The traffic, amazingly, wasn't too bad.
They arrived, in no-time, at their posh Mayfair pad;
A GORGEOUS, split-level, detached pied-à-terre
Where Little Miss Mary lived with-out a care.

And that's where we find her – tired from shopping,
Exhausted from all of that running and hopping,
From salon to boutique, with Mum as her caddie,
Buying up Bond Street and all on her Daddy...

Who works all day long, all night long in the City
As Chair Of The Board and the Head Of Committees;
Earning big bucks so that she can look pretty –
NO EXPENSE SPARED on his "Sweet Little Kitty".

Veni, Vidi, Vici - Armani, Fendi, Gucci!

Little Miss Mary made her Daddy proud
By jumping in queues and pushing through crowds,
By spending his money in ALL sorts of places
From Moscow to Paris, from Harrods to Macy's.

Mary would COME, she would SEE, she would BUY!
From Cannes to Hong Kong, from Milan to Dubai.
If there was a contest, then she would be crowned
"The world's greatest shopper!" (Yen, Dollars or Pounds).

But now she was tired and lay on her bed.
Musing if next season's black would be red.
Mulling the fate of poor fabric exporters
If all the designers cut skirts by three-quarters.

She put on her eye-mask and drifted to sleep;
Counting sheep, after sheep, after sheep, after sheep,
But all the while thinking: "How It would be better
To use all their wool for a Burberry sweater."

Soon Little Miss Mary was out like a light,
But she didn't sleep long and woke up with a fright!
She opened her eyes and was very surprised
When a huge, hairy Monster... MATERIALIZED!

The Monster yelled "BOO!" to give Mary a scare,
But Mary just fixed the great Beast with a stare.
She looked up and down from his toes to his hair
With total disdain while the Monster stood there.

"Why!" asked the Monster "You show me no fear!?"
"Have you looked in the mirror? You're just SO last year!
Your tail isn't bad, but is there a reason
For sporting those horns, which are just SO last season?

The Monster was stunned. At a loss what to say.
His prey wasn't screaming or running away!
He wasn't accustomed to such a response,
He was used to HYSTERICS not pert nonchalance.

But Mary stayed poised as a lady should be,
She displayed no attempt or desire to flee.
She turned on the light so that he could see clearer
And showed the big Monster his FACE in the mirror.

He gawked for a while at his wretched reflection,
He winced at his wrinkled and withered complexion.
"My skin feels like leather, I have crusty eyes!"
"What did you expect when you don't moisturize?"

“My nails are all broken! My teeth are all yellow!
My hair is in clumps!” He let out a BELLOW!
“My horns are askew and my fur coat is molting!”
He started to sob... “I am... truly... revolting!”

“Come on now, don’t cry.” Said Little Miss Mary.
“You DO have a choice, you don’t HAVE to be scary!
Behind that snarl and that piercing stare,
You’re just a big softy – a HUGE teddy-bear!”

But the big hairy Monster was not quite as certain –
Embarrassed he wrapped himself up in a curtain
And told Little Mary that with-out a doubt
He’s a HIDEOUS creature and he’ll NEVER come out!

Miss Mary agreed: “You are ugly for sure,
But it’s something you really don’t have to endure.
So you haven’t been blessed with the best of genetics;
Who needs Mother Nature, when we have cosmetics!?

For each of your problems you’ll find there’s a cure
From a deep cleansing facial to a French pedicure.
To NUMEROUS methods for rogue hair removal
So what do you say? Do I have your approval?

Would you like to be pampered and fashioned and styled?
MADE-OVER BY MARY?” – The big Monster smiled.

“I can tell from that smile that it’s been quite a while
Since you’ve seen a toothbrush, or have used a nail-file.
And I sense from your stench, or at least I presume,
That you’re also a stranger to soap and perfume.”

While Little Miss Mary stood pinching her nose
The big Monster blushed from his head to his toes.
“Don’t worry.” said Mary, “We’ll give you a shower
We’ll soak you and clean you, we’ll scrub and we’ll scour.

We’ll cleanse and we’ll tone, we’ll wax and we’ll pluck,
We’ll snip and we’ll peel, we’ll nip and we’ll tuck!
If you want to look pretty you’re on the right path.
Lets start with the basics... You’re having a bath!”

She DRAGGED the big Monster inside her en-suite
Full of lotions and potions all fragrant and sweet,
Full of loofahs and sponges to rub and to scrub
And rose scented candles lit round the tub.

Once there, the Monster forgot ALL his troubles
In bath salts and oils and white, fluffy bubbles.
And as he relaxed, Mary started her mission;
She began by shampooing and then she conditioned...

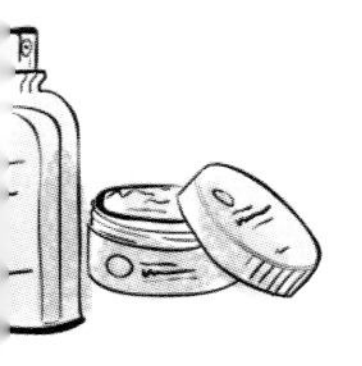

She used tinted toners, tonics and creams,
She applied elbow grease (as weird as it seems)
Because THAT, for Miss Mary, was EX-tremely rare.
After all, she was heir to a millionaire.

She rolled up her sleeves and got stuck in her task.
She smeared on a Dead Sea, firming face masque.
She lathered and foamed, she combed and untangled,
Till the Monster emerged spick'n'span and newfangled!

“Well there you go, you no longer smell foul.”
Said Little Miss Mary, handing over a towel.
“And now for the fun part, lets start from the top
To be brutally honest your hair is a MOP!

I have to be frank – I am not even sure
Of how to approach this kind of coiffure.
Maybe a fringe? Or a crop? Or a bob?
Or perhaps a French Plait will do just the job?

Whatever we do you will first have to swear;
In future you’ll take better care of your hair.
How on EARTH did you ever expect to make friends
With split-ends that have their OWN split-ends!?”

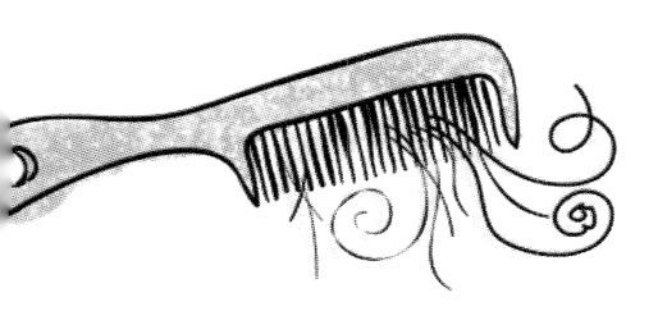

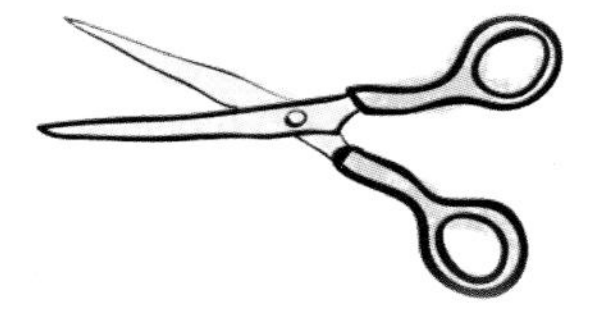

The Monster's face faded by at least several shades
Once he spotted the glint of the sharp scissor blades.
Frightened, he opted to keep his eyes shut
And chewed on his nails, through his first haircut.

Mary danced round his head like a crazed ballerina,
Like a MAD matador in a bullfight arena;
Dodging his horns while clipping his ears,
Which, it has to be said, only worsened his fears.

The Monster's anxiety did not diminish
Until Little Mary announced: "I AM FINISHED!"
He opened his eyes and was over the Moon!
It looked like his cut was by Vidal Sassoon!

His hair was no longer the nest of a vulture;
It was "modern-art" – like an avant-garde sculpture.
Geometric yet flowing. Organic yet neat...
And that's just the mound that lay at his feet!

"I'm so HAPPY Miss Mary I could give you a kiss!"
"While you have halitosis, I'll give that a miss;
There's still so much more that needs to be done.
Don't think this is over. The fun's JUST begun!"

Mary brushed up his teeth until they were white.
She polished his horns so they weren't such a fright.
She curled his eyelashes and buffed every nail.
She fluffed up his wings and she straightened his tail.

His immense monobrow was trimmed and then tweezed,
The spots on his nose were steamed and then squeezed,
She plucked his disgusting, unsightly nose hairs,
She peeled and exfoliated LOTS of skin layers...

With Caviar Granules for Derma-abrasion™
Which Mommy was saving for special occasions,
Who swore that the tiny, dried eggs from a Sturgeon
Were better than dating a TOP plastic surgeon.

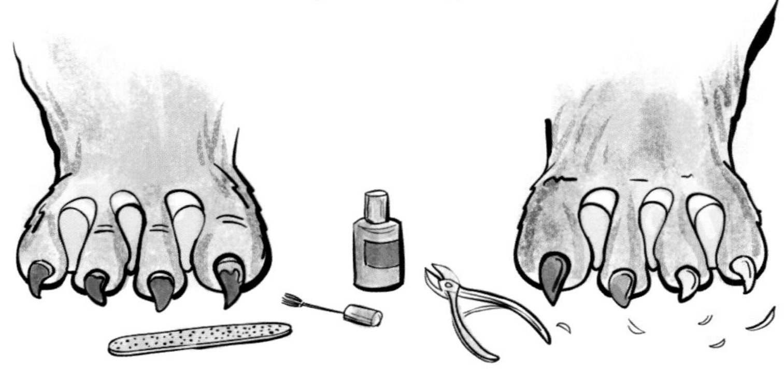

The results were AMAZING! Not a wrinkle in sight!
The Monster could hardly contain his delight.
He clapped his big hands and stomped his huge feet,
But Mary's makeover STILL wasn't complete!

She waited for calm and then said: "I suppose,
It's time that we found some suitable clothes.
My Daddy's quite fat, so I'm sure we can find
A suit that would fit your ENORMOUS behind."

They went to the wardrobe and opened the door
To haute-couture HEAVEN from ceiling to floor.
There were shoes, there were suits and dresses galore!
GAULTIER, GIVENCHY, CHANEL and DIOR!

The Monster was slack-jawed, his eyes open wide,
He hadn't the SLIGHTEST clue how to decide
Between: Prada, Armani or Gucci, or Boss.
In this maze of designers he was quite at a loss!

But thankfully Little Miss Mary was able
To find her way through the labyrinth of labels.
She scoured the shelves and rummaged through rails,
Convinced that the Monster would look great in tails...

Mary searched for her father's bespoke formal wear,
After all it was Daddy, who made her aware:
"That even a MONKEY dressed up in a tux
Has a GOOD chance to look like a million bucks."

She furnished the Monster with J.P. Tod's shoes,
A Ralph Lauren shirt, then proceeded to choose
A STUNNING tuxedo from Louis Vuitton
And with bated breath waited – as he put it on.

Within a few moments Miss Mary could tell
That the dressing-up part wasn't going so well.
It became pretty clear that the suit wouldn't fit
When the Monster bent down and his trousers split!

Propriety precludes me from telling you where,
But it was, as you guessed, an embarrassing tear.
The pants weren't designed for a beast of his size.
And the rest of the clothes met a likewise demise...

The tailor-made tailcoat was torn into shreds!
The shirt was reduced to some buttons on threads!
The waistcoat was wasted! The shoes were too small;
His toes burst right through them, but then, worst of all...

The Royal Ascot top hat, which was worn to the races,
Got impaled on the Monster's big horn of all places!
The final result meant the tux was in TATTERS...
The Monster had turned haute-couture into schmattas!

"I cannot believe I could be so naïve!"
Said Little Miss Mary a little bit peeved:
"I ought to have guessed it SOOO much faster
That getting you dressed would end in disaster!"

But the big hairy Monster was simply ecstatic,
He tingled all over (though it could have been static)
So what if his clothes were ripped at the seams?
They MORE than exceeded his WILDEST dreams!

“I want to thank you so much, just where do I start?
Instead of my gut, there’s a place in my heart
For Mary you’ve changed me both inside and out.
I was going to devour you... Now I’m DEVOUT.

I can’t wait to get back to the big monsters’ lair
To show them my clothes, my skin and my hair.
I shall teach other Monsters how not to be feared!”
He thanked her once more and with that... disappeared.

After waving good-bye Mary drew a deep sigh,
Lay back and imagined new things she could buy,
But hard as she tried her dreams weren't the same,
Compared to the Monster they all seemed so... tame.

Her entire short life she'd behaved like a brat
With "Can I have this?" and "Can I have that!"
But it looked like she'd finally found her passion;
Not JUST for herself, but for big monster fashion.

She never imagined one day she may yearn
Not for dresses or shoes, but a Monster's return.
When all of a sudden, she heard something creaking.
She sat up and listened to scraping and squeaking...

The closet doors opened and through them came out
A motley of monsters with horns, tails and snouts;
Sharp teeth and long tentacles, talons and trunks,
Some hairy, some scaly ALL smelly as skunks!

It's hard to find words to describe their features;
They were, beyond doubt, the UGLIEST creatures!
Every single one weird, every single one wild,
Every single one there to be fashioned and styled.

What do you do, when you're faced with such freaks?
Do you faint? Do you run? Do you hide? Do you shriek?
Miss Mary's solution was typically chic:
"I will open the world's first MONSTER BOUTIQUE!"

But that, I'm afraid, is a WHOLE different story,
I hope that you didn't think THIS part was boring,
After all, you have managed to get to the end,
Now, please recommend this book to a friend!

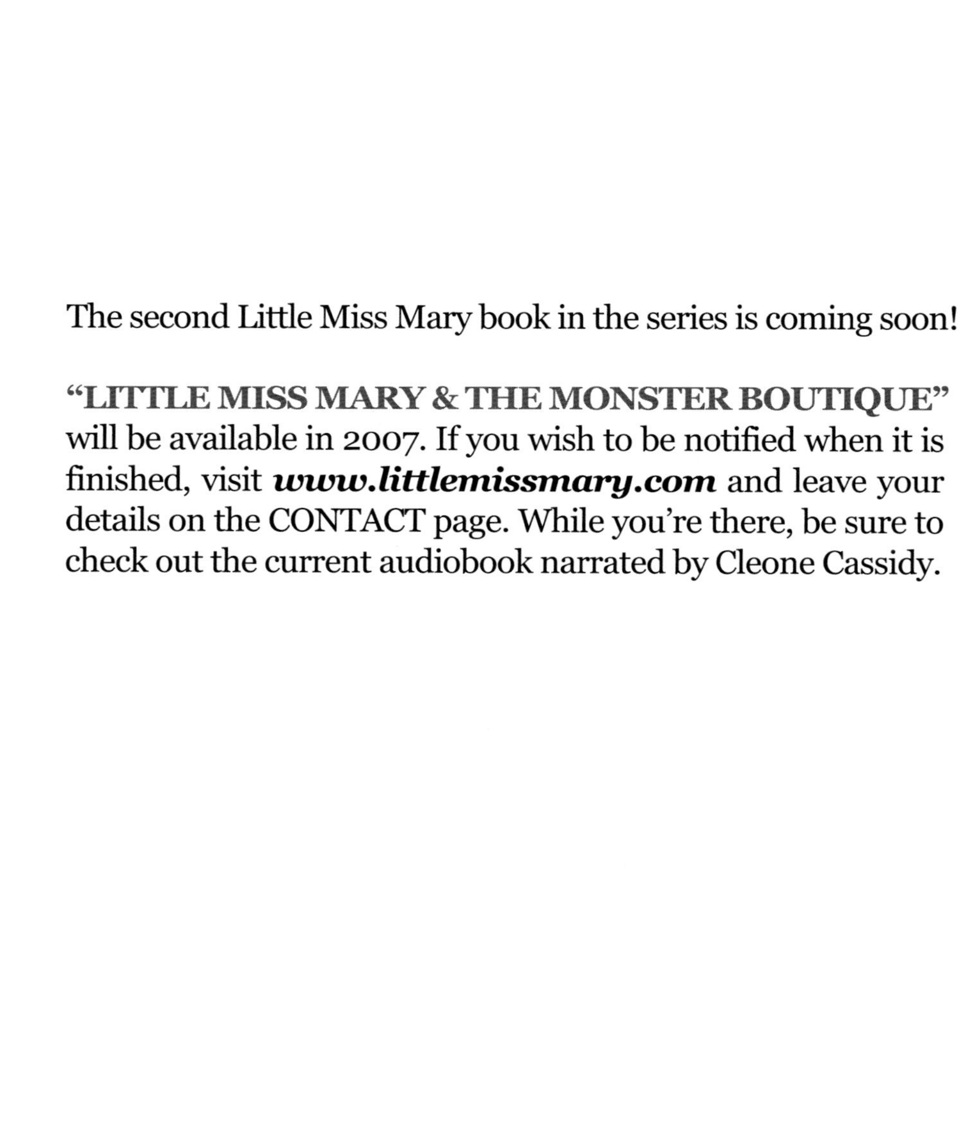

The second Little Miss Mary book in the series is coming soon!

"LITTLE MISS MARY & THE MONSTER BOUTIQUE" will be available in 2007. If you wish to be notified when it is finished, visit ***www.littlemissmary.com*** and leave your details on the CONTACT page. While you're there, be sure to check out the current audiobook narrated by Cleone Cassidy.

NEXT LINE
PUBLISHING

www.nextline.com
info@nextline.com

This book belongs to...